Acting Edition

Vladimir

by Erika Sheffer

ISBN 978-0-573-71184-8

www.concordtheatricals.com
www.concordtheatricals.co.uk

FOR PRODUCTION INQUIRIES

UNITED STATES AND CANADA
info@concordtheatricals.com
1-866-979-0447

UNITED KINGDOM AND EUROPE
licensing@concordtheatricals.co.uk
020-7054-7298

Each title is subject to availability from Concord Theatricals Corp., depending upon country of performance. Please be aware that *VLADIMIR* may not be licensed by Concord Theatricals Corp. in your territory. Professional and amateur producers should contact the nearest Concord Theatricals Corp. office or licensing partner to verify availability.

This work is published by Samuel French, an imprint of Concord Theatricals Corp.

No one shall make any changes in this title(s) for the purpose of production. No part of this book may be reproduced, stored in a retrieval system, scanned, uploaded, or transmitted in any form, by any means, now known or yet to be invented, including mechanical, electronic, digital, photocopying, recording, videotaping, or otherwise, without the prior written permission of the publisher. No one shall share this title(s), or any part of this title(s), through any social media or file hosting websites.

For all inquiries regarding motion picture, television, online/digital and other media rights, please contact Concord Theatricals Corp.

MUSIC AND THIRD-PARTY MATERIALS USE NOTE

Licensees are solely responsible for obtaining formal written permission from copyright owners to use copyrighted music and/or other copyrighted third-party materials (e.g. artworks, logos) in the performance of this play and are strongly cautioned to do so. If no such permission is obtained by the licensee, then the licensee must use only original music and materials that the licensee owns and controls. Licensees are solely responsible and liable for clearances of all third-party copyrighted materials, including without limitation music, and shall indemnify the copyright owners of the play(s) and their licensing agent, Concord Theatricals Corp., against any costs, expenses, losses and liabilities arising from the use of such copyrighted third-party materials by licensees. For music, please contact the appropriate music licensing authority in your territory for the rights to any incidental music.

IMPORTANT BILLING AND CREDIT REQUIREMENTS

If you have obtained performance rights to this title, please refer to your licensing agreement for important billing and credit requirements.

For my mother, Edith Sheffer.

VLADIMIR is an Edgerton Foundation New Play Commission awarded by Manhattan Theatre Club (Lynne Meadow, Artistic Director; Barry Grove, Executive Producer) and received its world premiere there on October 16, 2024. The production was directed by Daniel Sullivan, with scenic design by Mark Wendland, costume design by Jess Goldstein, lighting design by Japhy Weideman, original music and sound design by Dan Moses Schreier, projection design by Lucy Mackinnon, fight direction by Thomas Schall, hair and wig design by Charles G. LaPointe, makeup design by Ashley Ryan, dialect coaching by Charlotte Fleck, and casting by Caparelliotis Casting and Kelly Gillespie. The production stage manager was James FitzSimmons. The cast was as follows:

RAYA . . . . Francesca Faridany

KOSTYA . . . . Norbert Leo Butz

YEVGENY . . . . David Rosenberg

GALINA . . . . Olivia Deren Nikkanen

ANDREI . . . . Erik Jensen

JIM . . . . Jonathan Walker

CHOVKA . . . . Erin Darke

VLADIMIR was originally commissioned by Geffen Playhouse (Randall Arney, Artistic Director; Gil Cates Jr., Executive Director).

CHARACTERS

RAYA – a journalist, 40s–50s (Diminutive of RAISA)

KOSTYA – an editor, Raya's boss, 40s–50s (Diminutive of KONSTANTIN)

YEVGENY – a financial analyst, Raya's source, 30s (Diminutive: ZHENYA)

GALINA – Raya's daughter, 20s (Diminutive: GALYA)

ANDREI – a Kremlin official, Kostya's friend, 40s–50s

JIM – an American investor

CHOVKA – a young woman from Chechnya, teens–20s

The following doubling tracks were utilized in the premiere production:

YEVGENY/CAMERAMAN/SASHA

GALINA/DAUGHTER/MASHA/BARTENDER

ANDREI/DIRECTOR/DEACON

JIM/OLD MAN/VITALY/NEWS PERSONALITY

CHOVKA/MAKE-UP LADY/TATIANA/CREW MEMBER/CLERK

SETTING

Various locations in Moscow, Chechnya, and New York

TIME

Prologue: December 31, 1999

Part One: Spring 2004

Part Two: Fall 2004 to Winter 2005

NOTES ON DIALECT

Actors should use their native dialect: American, British, etc. Lines can be altered to suit the cadence of the actor's nationality. The exception is Jim, who is American and must speak with an American accent. Jim is always speaking English to non-native English speakers. When talking to Jim, actors use Russian-accented English, unless otherwise noted.

Jim speaks in an American dialect to identify him as a foreigner. You may find this theatrical device to be ineffective if the company's natural accents are too varied. If this is the case, unity of dialect is an option. Play around, find your way.

For we cannot tarry here,
We must march my darlings, we must bear the brunt of danger,
We the youthful sinewy races, all the rest on us depend...

"Pioneers! O Pioneers!"
Walt Whitman

PROLOGUE

(Moscow. December 31, 1999.)

(The **OLD MAN** *sits behind a desk, staring into the distance. He holds a glass of cognac. A TV camera is pointed at him. A* **DIRECTOR** *and the* **OLD MAN'S DAUGHTER** *loiter nearby.)*

(A Christmas tree. A military flag.)

VOICE. *(From control booth.)* Two minutes.

DIRECTOR. Okay, everyone, we have two minutes. Two minutes.

> *(The* **OLD MAN** *drinks.)*

The drink.

> *(**MAKE-UP LADY** approaches and attempts to remove the glass. But the* **OLD MAN** *keeps drinking. Takes his time.* **MAKE-UP LADY** *looks to* **DIRECTOR**, *unsure.)*

Mr. President. We have to start.

DAUGHTER. Daddy, it's starting.

Daddy.

DIRECTOR.	**DAUGHTER.**
He needs to get rid of the glass.	Give her the drink.
You don't want it there.	Can you –

DAUGHTER. I heard you! Daddy, give her the drink... Just give her the glass.

(The **OLD MAN** *finishes the drink and hands over the glass.* **MAKE-UP LADY** *passes it off.)*

DIRECTOR. Mariya, his forehead. Does he always sweat like – Can someone turn down the heat!

MAKE-UP LADY. It's not on.

DIRECTOR. Can someone turn on the A/C!

(As **MAKE-UP LADY** *is about to powder his forehead, the* **OLD MAN** *stands.)*

OLD MAN. I have to take a piss.

(Beat.)

DAUGHTER. Are you sure –?

DIRECTOR.	**DAUGHTER.**
We don't have time.	Can you hold it?

DIRECTOR. He won't make it back. We're live –

DAUGHTER. *(Vicious.)* I know that!

Daddy, you're going to have to hold it.

You have to. There's no time, every station is cutting to us, you have to hold it.

OLD MAN. I can make it back.

DAUGHTER. How far is the bathroom?

DIRECTOR. He won't make it.

DAUGHTER. How far is / the bathroom?

DIRECTOR. It's down the hall, it's a long hall, we have less than one minute.

DAUGHTER. There's really no time. I'm sorry.

DIRECTOR. He's not centered –

CAMERAMAN. He's standing.

(The **OLD MAN** *sits. He picks up a vase of flowers. He dumps the flowers and urinates into the vase, under the desk.)*

DIRECTOR. Thirty seconds. Mariya. His head.

*(***MAKE-UP LADY*** applies powder to the* **OLD MAN***'s head while he urinates. The* **OLD MAN** *finishes and holds the vase up to* **MAKE-UP LADY***.)*

Ten seconds.

*(***MAKE-UP LADY*** considers her options. She takes the vase, and exits.)*

Okay, everyone, deep breath. Five, four…

(He counts down silently and points to the **OLD MAN***.)*

OLD MAN. My dearest Russians. It is just a few moments before the most momentous date in history. The year 2000 is upon us. A new century, a new millennium.

This is the last time I will speak to you as your president.

I am resigning.

Russia must enter the next millennium with new faces, fresh voices, bright energetic men and women. History marches on and Russia will keep moving forward.

(A fuzzy image of the **OLD MAN** *appears, speaking in Russian as the actor continues in English.)*

And there is a good man waiting to lead you, a strong, courageous individual who will shape our future. And so, in accordance with our constitution, I have signed a decree handing over the duties of the president to my prime minister Vladimir Vladimirovich Putin.

(The vocals line up on the name. A feeling of an echo.)

OLD MAN. *(In Russian.)* Будьте счастливы, друзья мои. Вы заслуживаете счастья. Вы заслуживаете счастья и мира. *[Be happy my friends. You deserve happiness. You deserve happiness and peace.]*

DIRECTOR. *(In Russian.)* мы закончили *[...We're out.]*

PART ONE

One

(Projection:)   Moscow 2004.
                  Election Night.

(Raya's apartment. Living room and kitchen area. A hallway leads to the bedrooms. One of **RAYA***'s hands is in a cast up to the elbow and she has a bandage on her neck.)*

(On the television, a young Vladimir Putin gives a speech. The audio is in Russian. **RAYA** *sips a drink and watches the speech with contempt.)*

(The buzzer sounds. She presses the intercom.)

RAYA. Hello?

KOSTYA. *(Voice.)* It's Kostya.

RAYA. What are you doing here?

KOSTYA. I'm visiting. Open the door, it's freezing!

*(***RAYA*** buzzes him in. She pulls out an ice cube tray, but she's only got one hand for this maneuver. She slams the tray into the bowl. This doesn't work. Or it does!* **KOSTYA** *enters with* **TATIANA***, who is drunk. She's having trouble standing. He carries a ridiculously large vase of flowers.)*

KOSTYA. Here we are, two more steps.

TATIANA. I forgot my coat.

KOSTYA. You're wearing your coat.

TATIANA. I forgot my hat.

KOSTYA. Did you have a hat, I don't remember.

TATIANA. How can you not remember my hat? Do you even see me? Do you have any idea who I am?

KOSTYA. Darling, you're going to lie down for a bit all right?

RAYA. No.

KOSTYA. Just for a few hours, I couldn't get a car.

RAYA. Do not put her in there. Galina is here for the weekend.

KOSTYA. *(Changing direction.)* Okay.

RAYA. Don't put her in my room!

KOSTYA. She'll be fine in an hour, I promise –

(*To* **TATIANA**, *offstage.*) Darling, listen to me, you're going to lie down for a bit while I go find your hat –

TATIANA. *(Offstage.)* You won't.

KOSTYA. On my life –

TATIANA. Don't promise me things, you're always promising things and you never – Don't promise me anything ever again!

(*Beat.*)

I'm going to throw up.

RAYA. If she throws up in my bed, I will kill you –

KOSTYA. *(Re-entering.)* She already threw up twice, there's nothing left.

Well, my night took an unexpected turn...

RAYA. Why are you in my home with an embryo?

KOSTYA. She's not an embryo, her name is Tatiana and she's my new assistant.

>   *(Beat.)*

RAYA. Can't you just fuck them? Does it really require this much investment?

KOSTYA. You're being very judgmental. This aired hours ago.

RAYA. It's on a loop, they keep replaying it.

KOSTYA. That doesn't mean you have to watch, you still have use of your arms.

>   *(**RAYA** holds up her cast.)*

You have the other one.

RAYA. Where are you coming from?

KOSTYA. Khakamada's party.

RAYA. How was that?

KOSTYA. Very sad. They rented the Grand Ballroom at the Hilton.

RAYA. Why? She was polling at two percent.

KOSTYA. I have no idea, there were maybe twenty people there for her concession. Rows and rows of the saddest sushi you've ever seen. Beautiful centerpieces, though.

>   *(He displays the flowers.)*

RAYA. This is the fucking problem. This election is a joke, why is everyone playing along? The opponent rents a ballroom, gives a concession speech, as if there was even a possibility she would win. Why waste the fucking sushi?

KOSTYA. It was good sushi.

(**RAYA** *has become fixated on the screen.*)

RAYA. He ascends to the presidency like a fucking czar and four years later he steals an election – I bet his dick is so small.

(**KOSTYA** *pointedly turns off the TV.*)

KOSTYA. Hi.

RAYA. What?

KOSTYA. Your recovery might go a little smoother if you don't give yourself an aneurysm.

RAYA. It's infuriating.

KOSTYA. Okay, but what's the point of driving yourself crazy?

RAYA. It makes me feel better.

KOSTYA. It makes you feel fucking miserable.

RAYA. Yeah, but I like that feeling.

KOSTYA. You're acting like this is a surprise – Come on, look, Ivan the Terrible, pretty bad. Peter the Great, actually terrible. Lenin! He didn't bother with an election either. Stalin, Andropov, another KGB guy –

RAYA. So, because it's happened in the past, it makes it okay?

KOSTYA. No, but it makes it predictable.

How long is Galina in town for?

RAYA. God, too long.

KOSTYA. Stop it, she's the sweetest.

RAYA. Because you're not related to her. You don't know what it's like to be her mother. She's fucking relentless. She's treating me like an invalid. She stands outside the door when I go to the bathroom.

KOSTYA. Why?

RAYA. In case I fall in? I don't know.

I'm going into the office tomorrow.

KOSTYA. You said you'd take your full medical leave.

RAYA. It's a sprained wrist, a couple of burns, I don't need a month for that.

KOSTYA. It's more than a sprained wrist and you know it.

If you're sick of being at home, take a vacation, go sit on a beach somewhere.

RAYA. I have been back from Chechnya for three weeks. I have been a very good girl and it's time to go back to work.

KOSTYA. Okay.

RAYA. It's better if I'm at the office. I'll feel more relaxed, because I'm actually getting something done.

KOSTYA. Okay.

RAYA. Stop saying okay and say what you mean.

KOSTYA. Why don't we speed this up and you can just tell me what I mean?

RAYA. I know you think I should get a fucking massage and sit on my ass for two more weeks –

KOSTYA. Oh, that's what I think, okay.

RAYA. But I really don't have to.

KOSTYA. Then don't.

RAYA. You're not going to argue with me?

KOSTYA. I am not.

RAYA. Good. Because I have something to show you.

(She gets a file folder.)

KOSTYA. No, no, I'm not working right now.

RAYA. There is something here, I can feel it.

KOSTYA. Do not pitch me a story, I am barely sentient.

RAYA. So, my guy at the Tax Authority calls me last week, they got a complaint from an American. He owns an investment firm, small, boutique, name is James Kimball. He said someone used his company to claim a tax refund.

KOSTYA. I'm not listening to you.

RAYA. Guess how much the refund was for.

KOSTYA. No.

RAYA. Guess.

KOSTYA. ...A million rubles.

RAYA. Twenty million.

> *(Beat.)*

KOSTYA. Fuck. Let me see that. *(He peruses the documents.)* Did they open an investigation?

RAYA. No. The American called back the next day, said there was a mistake. *(Beat.)* The money got paid out. Twenty million rubles to an American company, to a tiny American company. It's the largest tax refund in Russian history. That kind of money doesn't get paid out unless someone at the top is getting a cut.

KOSTYA. You think Finance Minister?

RAYA. At least. But I wouldn't be surprised if it went higher.

KOSTYA. ...Okay, that might be something.

RAYA. I'll need to get the tax ID, follow the money – Can you have Darya send me everything on the American, I can try...

> *(**KOSTYA** turns on the radio to drown her out.)*

KOSTYA. Tomorrow.

RAYA. This is important.

KOSTYA. Nothing is important at this hour, especially not work.

RAYA. We're not working, we're talking.

KOSTYA. Talking doesn't involve paperwork.

RAYA. Kostya, I'm injured –

> (**KOSTYA** *sings along, finally breaking her resolve.*[*] *He pulls her in for a dance and she half-heartedly protests.*)

Oh my God, you stink of liquor.

> (**GALINA** *enters in her pajamas.*)

GALINA. What are you doing?

KOSTYA. My fault. I was nearby and couldn't get a car.

GALINA. *(To* **RAYA**.*)* You're supposed to take it easy.

RAYA. I'm three drinks into my night, how much easier do you want me to take it?

GALINA. And you're not supposed to drink with the painkillers.

KOSTYA. Drinking on painkillers actually improves efficacy. I've done extensive research.

GALINA. *(To* **KOSTYA**.*)* She doesn't need encouragement.

RAYA. She really doesn't.

GALINA. I'm not kidding.

RAYA. She's very serious.

---

[*] A license to produce *Vladimir* does not include a performance license for any third-party or copyrighted music. Licensees should create an original composition or use music in the public domain. For further information, please see the Music and Third-Party Materials Use Note on page iii.

GALINA. *(To* **KOSTYA.***)* Did she tell you she went into sepsis last week?

    (Beat.)

I got a call, your mother was found passed out at a bus stop. Her burns were infected. I had to get a last-minute flight, get my classes covered. They kept asking at the hospital how it happened, how she got a sulfur burn in the middle of Moscow. I should've given them *your* number. Have them arrest you instead.

KOSTYA. What did I do?

GALINA. You enable her.

RAYA. *(To* **KOSTYA***, re:* **GALINA.***)* I told you – Fucking relentless.

GALINA. If you weren't paying, arranging everything, she couldn't go. It's illegal for a journalist to even be in Chechnya on her own.

RAYA. I wasn't on my own, I was with an infantry division.

GALINA. That you abandoned on a regular basis.

RAYA. Well, I mean, yeah.

    (Beat.)

GALINA. Let me change your bandage while I'm up.

RAYA. It's fine.

GALINA. It's been four hours.

RAYA. I'll change it before I go to sleep.

GALINA. It's easier if someone else does it –

RAYA. If you want to spend the entire weekend nagging, you need to go stay with your father.

    (Beat.)

I'm sorry.

GALINA. It's fine.

RAYA. I'm just tired.

GALINA. *(To* **KOSTYA**.*)* Will you help her with the bandage, it's hard for her to reach – Use a Q-tip when you apply the cream, and you have to wear rubber gloves, the skin's exposed it could get reinfected. Are you drunk?

KOSTYA. I'm completely functional.

Hey, your mom told me about your engagement, congratulations.

(He gives her the centerpiece.)

GALINA. Thank you.

KOSTYA. When's the big day?

GALINA. October 20th.

KOSTYA. Coming right up.

GALINA. Don't say that, I have way too much to do, all of it in Peter, and I've been here every weekend, since she got back –

RAYA. You don't have to.

GALINA. It's for me as much as you.

RAYA. It's for you.

GALINA. Fine it's for me.

Don't let her stay up too late.

KOSTYA. I won't. I'm on my best behavior, promise.

*(***GALINA*** exits. ***KOSTYA*** washes his hands and gets the bandage and cream.)*

RAYA. I'm going back to Chechnya in a few weeks.

KOSTYA. Were you listening to any of that?

RAYA. She'll be fine. She'll get into her schoolwork, her friends. And I'll make it a short trip, two weeks tops.

KOSTYA. You just pitched me a story, a good one. Stay here and work on it.

RAYA. I can write two things at once, I'm very talented.

KOSTYA. We won't be able to clear you. It'll be impossible to find a unit for you to travel with.

RAYA. I want to go on my own this time.

KOSTYA. Jesus fucking Christ.

RAYA. Feds are too much trouble, they don't let you talk to anyone –

KOSTYA. Please don't ask me to help you get arrested, if not shot –

RAYA. I absolve you of all responsibility, you have nothing to do with it. You just have to pay for everything and run the story. You know it'll be good, you really want to pass that up? Kostya... Enable me.

KOSTYA. You should take a break.

RAYA. Is that vomit on your shirt?

KOSTYA. No.

RAYA. All right.

> *(Beat.)*

KOSTYA. Don't make me regret it, okay?

RAYA. Regret what?

KOSTYA. Paying for everything and running the story. Don't make me regret it.

> *(He pulls back her bandage, revealing a dark burn.)*

Two

(Lights shift as **RAYA** *gets her coat and* **KOSTYA** *exits.* **RAYA** *leaves the apartment and spots* **CHOVKA** *standing off to the side.)*

(Projection:)   Chechnya.

A memory.

RAYA. Hi.

*(***CHOVKA*** looks around, realizes* **RAYA** *is talking to her.)*

CHOVKA. Hi.

RAYA. Raisa Bobrinskaya. I'm with *Moscow Novosti*. It's a newspaper.

CHOVKA. Never heard of it.

RAYA. It's a Russian newspaper. Do you have a minute to talk?

CHOVKA. I don't talk to Russians.

RAYA. Totally understandable. I wouldn't either if I were you – Do you mind if I stand here? I'm waiting for my driver, he had to run an errand.

CHOVKA. Stand wherever you want.

RAYA. There was an explosion on the 217, IED. If you're waiting for someone it might be a while. It was all back roads this morning, we had to drive thirty kilometers around, which you know, for me it's fine, I get to meet people, listen to their stories... I'll stop talking.

CHOVKA. I don't think you will.

(They wait.)

RAYA. We could give you a ride. We're going to Grozny. I promise I'm harmless – well, irritating according to my daughter, but generally harmless.

CHOVKA. You're kinda funny.

RAYA. What's your name? It doesn't have to be your real name, just something you wouldn't mind me calling you.

CHOVKA. For your story? Do you think I'd be a good character, is that why you want to talk?

RAYA. I don't write about characters, I write about people.

CHOVKA. But sometimes you think of them as characters.

RAYA. I don't.

CHOVKA. Bullshit.

RAYA. I wouldn't be here, risking my life, if I thought of you as a character.

CHOVKA. Oh, so noble. You get paid for risking your life, that's a choice you made.

RAYA. It doesn't always feel like one.

　　　(Beat.)

CHOVKA. Is it worth it?

RAYA. Is what worth it?

CHOVKA. Doing something so utterly pointless with your life?

RAYA. It...it's not pointless.

CHOVKA. Are you sure?

RAYA. I...

CHOVKA. Just go home. We don't matter to anyone.

RAYA. You matter to me.

CHOVKA. Because you're actually here. But if I was on your television, some girl you saw for thirty seconds, would you really care about a war in a place you've never been to, maybe never heard of.

RAYA. No. I'd watch until it got too depressing and then change the channel. Unless. I saw a real person, who told me a real story. A person who made it so I couldn't look away.

CHOVKA. You're pretty good.

RAYA. Thank you.

CHOVKA. My name is Chovka.

RAYA. Raisa. Raya.

CHOVKA. There is something that happened. Something I haven't talked about... I lost my heart. About a year ago.

RAYA. You lost heart.

CHOVKA. No, no, my heart. The organ. The thing that pumps your blood. I don't have one of those anymore.

RAYA. What does that mean?

(*A car horn.*)

CHOVKA. Your driver's back.

RAYA. What?

(**RAYA** *looks out, and* **CHOVKA** *exits.*)

Wait! Wait, what does that mean?

(**RAYA** *exits.*)

Three

(Light shift as **KOSTYA**, **ANDREI**, *and* **VITALY**
*enter with drinks and take a seat in a swanky
bar.)*

ANDREI. People don't mind getting fucked as long as you
use the right lubricant.

KOSTYA. That's what you tell yourself so you can sleep at
night.

VITALY. What's the right lubricant? I know it's metaphorical
lubricant, but what, like how?

ANDREI. I sleep great. Last night I dreamt I was a matador
– I'm in the ring with this bull, he's charging and I trip
on my bejeweled slipper. I back up and hit the wall.
Bull stops, we share a meaningful exchange and I can
feel it. *This bull wants me.* I'm breathing heavy, my
amygdala's fucking gyrating –

KOSTYA. And you consider this a good night's sleep.

ANDREI. Well, then he sucks my cock and I wake up
feeling great. Made blinis from scratch, squeezed fresh
orange juice, my wife was elated.

KOSTYA. She was probably grateful to the bull. Freed up
her morning.

VITALY. Andrei Vodka-vich, Konstantin Cognac-ovich –

KOSTYA. Vitaly Full-of-shit-ovich, have a seat so I can
stop staring at that massive gut.

ANDREI. It's a beauty.

KOSTYA. Just when I'm convinced no time has passed
since university, I'm confronted with this decrepit
specimen.

ANDREI. God, when did we get so old?

KOSTYA. *(Raising his glass.)* As always, gentlemen. A pleasure.

VITALY & ANDREI. Cheers, hear, hear, etc.

(They drink.)

KOSTYA. Andrei Karlovich, tell me, what nefarious dealings have you been involved with, lately?

ANDREI. No comment.

KOSTYA. Oh, come on, I've been watching the news.

ANDREI. Why would I tell you anything? So, I can see it twisted around –

KOSTYA. Reported on –

ANDREI. In that pathetic little rag. Nasty, biased –

KOSTYA. Journal. Independent journal.

ANDREI. Let's stick to sports and family –

KOSTYA. I'm sorry, I can't show up to work, look my staff in the eye if I don't at least get a comment on governor appointments.

ANDREI. The Kremlin is pleased that rival parties were able to put politics aside and act in the public's best interest.

KOSTYA. That's what you're going with?

VITALY. That was good. That was really good.

KOSTYA. Three months ago you didn't have the votes to bring it to committee, now it's unanimous? Suddenly having the president appoint governors makes more sense than people actually voting for them.

ANDREI. When you look at local corruption, the bribes –

KOSTYA. *(To* **VITALY.***)* I'll tell you why he's brilliant. And an asshole. But brilliant, first. Because he knows people want the show. They could've brought the bill up, pushed it through on day one, but no. We get months of debates, counter bills, talk show appearances, public declarations about how and why every last idiot changed his mind. Meanwhile, it was a forgone conclusion. Wasn't it?

ANDREI. Since when is public debate a bad thing? Last I checked it was a key feature of democracy.

KOSTYA. When it's legitimate. When everyone's arguing, but they all know the ending – That's not democracy, that's theater.

ANDREI. You think it's any different in Europe, America? You think their politicians don't have a script, people don't know exactly what's going to come out of their mouths? We don't do anything the rest of the world doesn't do. For some reason we're the only ones getting blamed for it.

KOSTYA. And that's why he's an asshole. Not only does he fuck you over, he complains about how much he suffered doing it.

ANDREI. Why do you even need a comment – You're so good at inventing them.

KOSTYA. I don't invent / comments.

ANDREI. Fabricating conflict when there's nothing there.

KOSTYA.	**ANDREI.**
You want to lie to the public, fine, but not to me, we've known each other too long.	It's all smoke. But it sells. Oh. Wait. It doesn't even do that.

ANDREI. What's your circulation?

VITALY. Is anyone hungry, or are we just –

KOSTYA. It's up from last year, two point one percent.

ANDREI. He counts the point one, that's adorable.

KOSTYA. It's not just a question of sales – Raisa Bobrinskaya has been picked up by the AP four times in the past year.

ANDREI. That fucking Judas.

 (Beat.)

Our boys are freezing in the woods, she makes them sound like animals, war criminals – They're kids.

KOSTYA. Those boys wouldn't be missing their families, if your boss didn't want them there.

ANDREI. But he's not biased –

KOSTYA. Your guy needs chaos, Andrei. But it's gotta be at the border – far enough that it doesn't affect anyone, but he can still point to it and say, "I'm a tough guy, I'm really doing things over here."

ANDREI. What do you think happens if we pull out? You think they'll raise their chickens and leave us the fuck alone? Sorry, if I don't feel like trusting terrorists.

KOSTYA. They're just people, Andrei, like you and me –

ANDREI. Jesus, you sound just like her. *(Raises his glass.)* To Raisa Bobrinskaya, patron saint of the suicide bomber. May her life be long and end in a burst of excitement!

 *(**ANDREI** drinks.)*

I'm surprised you've kept her on this long. It's not like you don't have other options.

KOSTYA. No one as good, no one as / willing to –

ANDREI. She's a shit stirrer. And a terrible writer. You ever notice how everyone talks about how important she is, but no one actually reads her? I've tried. The eye just glazes.

I'm sure she'd find something if you let her go. You'd both benefit, she'd go to New York, London, you'd be less...exposed. Have you thought about it?

KOSTYA. I haven't.

ANDREI. Huh... And here I thought you were a smart guy.

> (**RAYA** *enters another, less swanky bar and sees* **YEVGENY** *having a drink alone.*)

RAYA. Rough day?

YEVGENY. The usual. Work stuff.

RAYA. That's actually what I wanted to talk to you about.

YEVGENY. Excuse me?

RAYA. Raisa Bobrinskaya. I'm with *Moscow Novosti.*

> (*Beat.*)

YEVGENY. Oh, fuck.

RAYA. I've been trying to reach you, I don't know if you got my messages.

YEVGENY. Yes. And I didn't return them because I have nothing to say. Please stop. I don't have any information, I swear.

RAYA. Okay, I totally understand. I'll stop right this minute.

> (*Beat.*)

Do you mind if I sit here? I could use a drink.

YEVGENY. ...Sit wherever you want.

> (*She looks to the* **BARTENDER.**)

RAYA. I'll have a cognac.

So, where are you from originally –?

YEVGENY. Oh my God...

RAYA. I just thought I heard an accent.

YEVGENY. I'm from Ukraine. Mukachevo.

RAYA. I've taken that train ride before. When you come over the mountains it's so wild, like you're stepping back in time. What brought you all the way here?

YEVGENY. University. Moscow State.

RAYA. That's an accomplishment.

YEVGENY. I know what you're doing. You want me to let my guard down so I'll talk to you, but I swear I don't know anything.

RAYA. You're not the only one. When I called the Tax Authority, no one there knew anything either. Which is strange because I was asking about the largest tax refund in Russian history. And it's owned by an American? You'd think someone would know *something* about a payout of twenty million rubles. But no. Not the agency who issued the payment. And apparently not the chief accountant of the company who received it.

YEVGENY. We never saw a kopek of that money.

RAYA. So, it just disappeared?

YEVGENY. Wouldn't be the first time.

(Beat.)

RAYA. Your boss filed a complaint with the Tax Authority. He claimed someone used his name to register shell companies in Siberia.

YEVGENY. That complaint was rescinded. And confidential.

RAYA. A little bird told me about it.

YEVGENY. I'm going to tell you what I told my boss: Don't go looking for trouble, because it's never good when you find it.

RAYA. It doesn't bother you that someone can defraud our country of millions and just get away with it?

YEVGENY. It's none of my business.

RAYA. It's entirely your business. And mine. That money's meant to pay for schools, pensions. It's your money, my money – Do you have children?

YEVGENY. No, uh, almost. I'm about to.

RAYA. Congratulations.

YEVGENY. Thank you.

RAYA. Do you feel any obligation to this unborn child to make the world a better place?

YEVGENY. I thought you reported on the war.

RAYA. This is part of it.

YEVGENY. It's tax crime.

RAYA. It's power. We've been at war for eight years, and I know it doesn't feel like it because you can still go to the mall and the movies, and it's not even *called* a war. But it is. And the people who are sending troops off to murder children and bomb hospitals are the same ones using this country like a personal bank account. The thing about power is it needs fuel. Money is the fuel.

(*Beat.*)

YEVGENY. Look, I'm sorry.

RAYA. How about we just talk? Get to know each other.

YEVGENY. Why?

RAYA. Because you're still sitting here.

YEVGENY. Maybe I just want to finish my drink.

RAYA. Yeah, maybe...

(Beat.)

Why did you stay in Moscow after school? It's a long way from home.

YEVGENY. I met my wife, her family is here. And there weren't a lot of finance jobs where I'm from.

RAYA. Weren't a lot of finance jobs anywhere back then.

YEVGENY. Being an accountant was basically being a bookkeeper.

RAYA. Being a journalist was basically being a stenographer.

(They share a laugh.)

YEVGENY. That reminds me of a joke. A man goes to his local KGB office to report that his talking parrot is missing. Officer says, "We don't handle that, you have to go to the criminal police." Man says, "I will, of course. I just want *you* to know that I disagree with the parrot."

RAYA. Okay here's one. An American dog, a Polish dog and a Russian dog sit together. The American dog says, "In my country, if you bark, they'll give you meat." Polish dog says, "What is meat?" And the Russian dog says, "What is bark?"

See? Apathy.

YEVGENY. I don't think we're apathetic.

RAYA. We just have no problem with a sham election, a grinding war that we're losing and have no moral right to be in –

YEVGENY. Jesus –

(**YEVGENY** *looks around nervously. Anyone can be listening. The* **BARTENDER** *glances their way with suspicion.*)

RAYA. See, you don't even want to hear it out loud. No one does.

YEVGENY. Not because I'm apathetic.

RAYA. So you do care.

YEVGENY. Of course I do, I've – I've read your book, and some of your articles, and it's terrible what's happening over there. Especially the kids you write about. But come on, what am I supposed to do?

RAYA. This is what I'm talking about, apathy.

YEVGENY. I'm not apathetic, I'm afraid.

RAYA. You think you're afraid, because you've been trained to be.

YEVGENY. What's the difference between thinking you're afraid and actually being afraid?

RAYA. You get to be afraid when something is happening. When it's not happening, it's just an excuse not to do anything.

YEVGENY. I'm sorry, when has getting involved in this country ever been anything other than a terrible idea?

RAYA. When it's the right thing to do.

(*Back to* **KOSTYA.**)

ANDREI. I'm telling you this as a concerned party – You're wasting your best years at that paper. I don't know if I can keep coming out, if *both* of you are total failures.

VITALY. I might not join you guys next time, I'm seriously considering that.

KOSTYA. You've hurt his feelings.

ANDREI. Shit, have I?

VITALY. Fuck you.

KOSTYA. He's suffering. Clearly.

ANDREI. Do you need a hug? I can get someone to hug you, if you need a hug.

VITALY. I'm going to the bathroom.

> (**VITALY** *starts to go.*)

KOSTYA. Vitalya, come on.

ANDREI. Wait a minute. / Hey, hey.

VITALY. What – What is it?

ANDREI. If you see the waiter, tell him to bring more zakuski.

VITALY. I might genuinely hate you. I can't even tell anymore.

> (**VITALY** *exits.* **ANDREI** *lights a cigarette.*)

KOSTYA. I thought Sveta made you quit after your heart attack.

ANDREI. It was a cardiac event. And she did. I only do it after eight p.m.

KOSTYA. Good, I hear it only kills you if you do it in the morning.

Are you planning something?

ANDREI. Like what?

KOSTYA. Criticizing who I work with, telling me to get a new job. I'm just wondering if you know something I don't.

ANDREI. I know lots of things you don't.

KOSTYA. There are people who work for me who have families. If they need to start looking, I'd like to give them a heads up.

ANDREI. You're the editor, if anyone knows the state of your independent journal it's you.

KOSTYA. If you're planning on shutting us down – I consider you a friend, I would think you'd give me a little notice.

ANDREI. We don't shut down news outlets.

KOSTYA. Okay, I'll be more specific: Are you planning on raiding our offices? Am I being investigated for tax fraud? Do you have a tape of me with a couple of hookers dressed like Nazis?

ANDREI. Do you ever meditate?

KOSTYA. Go fuck yourself.

ANDREI. What you're experiencing now, this suffering – The Buddha would say that you've attached yourself to a fixed reality, when there is only change, there is only Impermanence.

KOSTYA. If you could correlate your words to meaning for once, I would be so grateful.

ANDREI. I've known you for a long time and I've never known you to be an idiot. As your friend. I'm telling you. Don't start now. Your election coverage did not go unnoticed. The way you've handled the war –

KOSTYA. The way I've handled –

ANDREI. It's a betrayal, it really is.

KOSTYA. We haven't printed anything that wasn't true.

ANDREI. Did you just roll out of a fucking cabbage patch – Who gives a shit? Truth gets decided in hindsight. And every fifty years we all get to change our minds about it. Kostya, look around you. Moscow Sechas, RBC. You think it will end with them? You think your boss is immune?

KOSTYA. I thought you didn't shut down news outlets.

ANDREI. They're not shut down. They're just under new management. Make a choice, Kostya. Before someone makes it for you.

(Back to **RAYA**. *The* **BARTENDER** *puts the check on the bar.)*

RAYA. I didn't ask for that.

BARTENDER. I know who you are. We don't serve degenerates.

RAYA. That must cut into your profit margin.

BARTENDER. Are you going to leave or do I have to get my manager?

RAYA. Get your manager.

YEVGENY. Don't, please, we're leaving.

RAYA. I want to meet her manager, I'm single, this could be the start of something exciting.

YEVGENY. I'm sorry if we were loud, we're going. Right now.

RAYA. Wouldn't want you to have to serve a drink to just anyone. I can't imagine the horror.

YEVGENY. *(To* **BARTENDER**.*)* Thank you. Sorry.

(The **BARTENDER** *exits.* **RAYA** *pulls out her card.)*

RAYA. You know what off the record means, right?

YEVGENY. Yeah, it means I get fucked later rather than right now.

RAYA. Anything could be helpful. Just think about it.

(Beat.)

YEVGENY. You know when I was a kid and something unfair happened, some thug tripped me in the courtyard, or a teacher failed me, gave me the Jew grade, I would imagine a metal band around my throat. I could feel it tightening just as I was about to speak up. My throat would get smaller and smaller, until it was a bean, a piece of gravel.

That's not apathy. I don't know what it is, but it's not apathy.

> *(He takes her card and exits. Alone, **RAYA** lets down her guard, suddenly exhausted by the encounter. She seems to have a headache. She goes back to the bar and downs the rest of her drink as **CHOVKA** appears.)*

CHOVKA. You should drink less.

RAYA. *(Sputtering.)* Oh, God... You sound like my daughter.

CHOVKA. Is she very smart?

RAYA. She is. She's studying in St. Petersburg. She's about your age, getting married in a few months.

CHOVKA. You must be busy.

RAYA. She's pretty self-sufficient.

CHOVKA. Why do you tell yourself that?

> *(Beat.)*

Looks like you found a new character. I think he'll be a good one. Unassuming, working man.

RAYA. He's not a character.

CHOVKA. You're right, he's not. You sure you want him to call you back? People who call you back don't tend to... thrive.

RAYA. That has nothing to do with me.

CHOVKA. Doesn't it?

> *(Beat.)*

RAYA. Are you still alive?

CHOVKA. Maybe you'll find out on your next trip back.

> *(Beat.)*

RAYA. What did you mean before? When you said you lost your heart?

CHOVKA. Oh. I meant there's nothing in here now.

RAYA. What happened to it?

CHOVKA. A bird ate it.

RAYA. Huh.

CHOVKA. Do you want to know what kind of bird?

RAYA. It wasn't my first question.

CHOVKA. It was a crow. Last year, during Ramadan, the whole village was sitting down to breakfast. And there was an air strike. Killed my mother, my brother, my uncle and...three cousins. I was in our house those first few weeks, devastated, totally numb, and one day a bird flew in through the window, and started talking. I know. Weird. It said, Do you miss walking, being outside? I thought, No, that sounds completely exhausting. Do you miss sunshine and the taste of sweet things? Nope. He says, well what do you miss? And I thought... I miss anticipation.

I miss the chance that something good will happen. Not even in the future, just later today, in an hour.

Crow says, You have to cure yourself. Of hope. And hope is big, it's the most valuable thing a person can own.

And I think, Yes. Cure me.

CHOVKA. He hopped over to right here *(She points at her chest.)* and pierced my chest. He tunneled through my muscles, nibbling, devouring. He ate my heart, and then he just...flew out the window.

RAYA. And now you're hopeless.

CHOVKA. Completely

(**CHOVKA** *exits.*)

Four

*(Jim's office. **JIM** sits at his desk, wearing a headset. He's on a call. **YEVGENY** and **MASHA** speak with and without Russian accents, as noted. They stand by the entrance to the office.)*

JIM. *(On the phone.)* He said that to you? He said that to your face?!

*(**YEVGENY** addresses **MASHA**.)*

YEVGENY. *(No accent.)* I'll come back when he's off the phone.

MASHA. *(No accent.)* He told me he was ready for you.

YEVGENY. *(No accent.)* Come get me when he's done.

MASHA. *(No accent.)* Oh, *that's* my job? Getting people?

YEVGENY. *(No accent.)* I'm working on my budget report and he's busy –

JIM. *(On the phone.)* Listen to me, he's gonna get in your face, let you know he owns you, which is *bullshit*. So, what I need from you, is to get there first. You walk out there and *you* set the terms. You level him, you eat his guts with a goddamn pair of chopsticks! ...Okay, kiddo, go ahead and put your mom on – *(He motions for **YEVGENY** to sit.)* Have you had coffee?

YEVGENY. *(With accent.)* Is fine, I don't need.

JIM. It's my son's last game of the season. Have something, water, tea – Masha, can you get him something?

MASHA. *(With accent.)* Why he can't get, he know where is.

JIM. Can you just ask him what he wants and get it? *(On the phone.)* Hey, sweetie, no, I'm here...

MASHA. *(To* **YEVGENY,** *no accent.)* Hey, Yevgeny, can I do something for you that you're totally capable of doing?

YEVGENY. *(No accent.)* No, thank you.

MASHA. *(No accent.)* 'Cause I can miss my train and can get home forty minutes later, you just say the word.

YEVGENY. *(No accent.)* I'm good.

JIM. Did you tell him we have croissants?

MASHA. *(With accent.)* Yeah. I tell him.

> (**JIM** *gives* **YEVGENY** *a thumbs up.* **MASHA** *exits.)*

JIM. *(On the phone.)* Honey, its pregame jitters, he'll be fine – Just plenty of Gatorade, okay? Love you, too, bye.

> (**JIM** *removes the headset, stretches out with a groan.* **YEVGENY** *speaks with an accent for the remainder of the scene.)*

I've got this twenty-minute window to catch New York before they leave for school.

YEVGENY. I didn't know your kids was so young.

JIM. Yeah, Sam's twelve, Ryan's eight. They were here at first, but my wife couldn't get used to the, uh...*culture*... So. Yevgeny.

YEVGENY. Mr. Kimball.

JIM. Jim. Please.

YEVGENY. Okay.

JIM. I'm not gonna sugarcoat this – We lost another client this morning. That's our third in three weeks. You said to close the investigation, you said don't complain, it'll be worse for us if we stir shit up. From where I'm sitting, it's looking pretty bad.

YEVGENY. What reason they give you for leaving?

JIM. Fuckin' going in a new direction – These guys are getting poached! And I can't blame them. How are they supposed to trust me with their money, when someone stole my fucking name and I just roll over. It's zebra shit, I can't believe I'm doing it.

YEVGENY. I'm not familiar... Zebra shit?

JIM. Okay. A lion looks out at the plain, decides what he's gonna eat, and fuckin' eats it. A zebra is an herbivore. Nobody wants a fuckin' herbivore managing their portfolio.

YEVGENY. We don't know who is stealing company information. Claim was filed from Siberia. Who knows who these people are? We go looking, we could find someone dangerous – Mafia, maybe.

JIM. The Siberian mafia? What do they, have the reindeer market locked up?

YEVGENY. Mr. Kimball.

JIM. Jim.

YEVGENY. Jim. Is better in this country sometimes to mind your own business. It's safer.

JIM. Don't take this the wrong way, but you're Jewish, aren't you?

(*Beat.*)

YEVGENY. Um...

JIM. You want to know how I can tell?

(*Beat.*)

YEVGENY. ...Okay.

JIM. When someone has to face that kind of adversity, you end up working twice as hard, three times as hard – You have to or there's no way you'd have made it. I don't pretend to know anything about what you've gone through in this country, but I do have the slightest, I mean a fraction of an idea – Listen, my internship interviews? It was like an Aryan fuckfest. Every Chip, Mitch, and Winston passed on me that year. Those walls are high, no matter where you're from.

(Pause.)

YEVGENY. Oh, you're Jewish.

JIM. Yeah.

YEVGENY. Ah, okay.

JIM. You couldn't tell?

YEVGENY. Your name don't sound.

JIM. My mom's side. The side that counts. All I'm saying is I know you've had to work hard to get here. But you're here now. *Own it.*

YEVGENY. You are in Russia few years, Jim. You know this country is difficult system, is not fair.

JIM. It's more fair than America. At least here, *everybody* gets fucked. It's egalitarian when you think about it. You think you don't have to pay to play in the States? You gotta pay tuition, your dad has to buy a building, pay your rent so you can take an internship. Man, I respect your country. At least you guys are up front about it.

YEVGENY. It's very "up front." You know why I'm older than all analyst in my department? Is taking me four years to get into university.

JIM. You? No fuckin' way.

YEVGENY. Yeah...fucking way. First year, I'm doing well on my exam, I think they can't say no – But they call me in for interview, there is few more questions they have – You know Goldbach conjecture?

JIM. Sure.

YEVGENY. Man give me problem on paper.

JIM. It's unsolvable.

YEVGENY. This what I tell him. No one can solve. He say, "Does not matter no one can solve. Only matter, *you* cannot solve." This called coffin question. Because that's where it puts you. Same thing, next year. Twin prime conjecture – Impossible. Third year, I go to education office, and two boys from my school are there. They say, "You really think you deserving place over a real Russian?" And they knock me down, punch me. Fourth year, I get lucky.

Now, if I complain, what you think happen, ah? You think I'm getting in?

JIM. No.

YEVGENY. This what I think, too.

But I wonder some time, what if this okay? And I start to imagine this life where I don't go back for beating. Life where I don't go back four times to get something which I deserve from beginning. Yeah, I imagine what kind of man this is.

JIM. He's a lion.

YEVGENY. Yeah... He's a lion.

(Pause. **JIM** *roars.)*

JIM. You do it.

YEVGENY. Do what?

JIM. Be a lion.

YEVGENY. Oh. Uh. No, thank you.

JIM. Are you a fuckin' zebra, Yevgeny? Or are you a lion?

YEVGENY. These are my choices?

JIM. Yeah.

YEVGENY. Okay. Then I am lion.

JIM. Are you sure about that?

YEVGENY. Yes. Yes, I am lion.

JIM. You are.

YEVGENY. I am.

JIM. You're a lion!

YEVGENY. I am lion!

JIM. You're a lion!

YEVGENY. I am lion!

> (**JIM** *roars.* **YEVGENY** *roars back. They both roar.*)
>
> (*Pause.*)

I should go back to my desk.

JIM. All right. Get back to me about next steps.

YEVGENY. Uh-huh...

> (**YEVGENY** *heads to the door. He turns back.*)

Uh, Jim?

JIM. Yeah?

YEVGENY. Send me to Siberia. I'm going to find out who stole the money.

Five

(Raya's apartment. **GALINA** *addresses wedding invitations, while* **RAYA** *looks through the cupboards.)*

RAYA. Where did you put the tea?

GALINA. I didn't touch it.

RAYA. When you live alone things are where you put them. It's company that's really the variable.

GALINA. Do you want me to go home early because you can't find your tea?

RAYA. I didn't say that.

GALINA. You basically said that. Did you look behind stuff?

*(***RAYA** *finds her tea behind other things. She flips the kettle on and gets out a tea bag.)*

RAYA. I don't keep it behind stuff.

(They share a smile.)

GALINA. We're having a party in St. Peter for everyone who can't make it to the wedding. Maybe after New Year's? Will you be back from your book tour by then?

RAYA. I don't know if I'll even go.

GALINA. Mom, it's a trip to America. And they're paying. You have to promote your book.

RAYA. Honey, these things are pathetic. You show up at a bookstore, there are maybe thirty people, less if it's raining. They ask questions to show how smart they are, how they care about the right things. Then everyone leaves feeling very good about themselves, and nobody does anything. It's like they think the reading is the doing. The whole thing is just...disappointing.

GALINA. Maybe your presence will inspire someone.

RAYA. Why do you mess with me?

GALINA. Because you deserve it.

RAYA. How's the planning going?

GALINA. It's coming along. Sasha's mother is meeting with the florist and the caterer this weekend.

RAYA. It's good she's helpful.

GALINA. She's...interesting.

RAYA. What does that mean?

GALINA. God, the other day she said I needed to work on my walk. That it wasn't sexy enough. I mean, she was kind of motherly about it.

RAYA. That's not a statement you can be motherly about.

GALINA. She said I needed to imagine a cherry up my butt.

RAYA. What?!

GALINA. She made me do it with her.

RAYA. You didn't.

GALINA. I did. It was really weird.

RAYA. I'll never understand women like that.

GALINA. I'm sure she thinks about it in terms of happiness, like if they're more attractive, they'll have better choices. They're basically her whole life.

(The apartment buzzer buzzes.)

RAYA. Your papa's mother was like that. Hello?

KOSTYA. *(Voice.)* It's Kostya.

RAYA. You're too young to remember, she was always telling me how I could do things the way he liked them – Don't do that. Make your whole world about being a wife. I promised myself I would never be that person.

GALINA. Not to worry, you succeeded.

RAYA. You're lucky I did. If I'd have been home more, can you imagine what kind of fruits I'd tell you to put up your butt?

GALINA. She's not that bad, she's actually very welcoming.

RAYA. Who'd she vote for?

GALINA. I didn't ask.

RAYA. But you know.

GALINA. Don't be rude to her at the wedding.

RAYA. Fucking idiot.

GALINA. Mom.

RAYA. Don't worry. If I treated idiots the way they deserved, I'd never get through my day. Hi, you're freezing.

(**KOSTYA** *enters with a bakery box.*)

KOSTYA. It feels like January, it's awful. For my sweets.

GALINA. Kostya, promise you'll make her behave at the wedding.

RAYA. She's worried about how I'll be with Sasha's family.

KOSTYA. What's wrong with Sasha's family?

RAYA.	**GALINA**.
His mother sounds dumber than a bag of hair.	Nothing –

GALINA. She disagrees with you, how is that a crime?

RAYA. I'm all for open discourse, but is everything up for debate? Is genocide up for debate?

GALINA.	**KOSTYA**.
Oh, my God, you are so –	No one's even going to offer me a drink.

GALINA. This is why you don't have friends.

KOSTYA. She has friends.

GALINA. She has colleagues, it's different. No one has to make an effort to see her, she's just there, like the weather.

RAYA. Sweetheart, I'm fine not having friends. All friends do is eat your food and drink your liquor, I found someone to do that and he pays me.

KOSTYA. *(To* **RAYA.***)* She's not wrong, you know.

GALINA.	**RAYA.**
Thank you.	What?

KOSTYA. You should try to communicate with people who think differently than you.

RAYA. Why?

KOSTYA. If you don't, we're at an impasse as a society –

RAYA. This country was born at an impasse.

RAYA.	**KOSTYA.**
It should've been written into the constitution. "This is never going to work, but let's come up with some rules we can ignore together."	So unless you want to roll out the tanks –

KOSTYA. Okay, here's a reason. As your friend, as someone who genuinely cares for you, for whom this actually matters –

RAYA. This will be good, listen to the build up.

KOSTYA. Intractability is a terrible quality in a journalist.

RAYA. So are alcoholism and syphilis, but you seem to be doing just fine.

KOSTYA. Fucking forget it.

GALINA. Don't argue with her, it's like a black hole, she'll suck the life out of you

RAYA. You think I don't know his family, I know them, shitty apartment, shared kitchen, waiting in line for meat, sugar, and now that feels distant, and if someone has to suffer, fine as long as it's someone far away. You want me to stand in a room and smile at that kind of complacency? Forget it. And if that means I have to leave your wedding, fine, because it is the last place I want to be.

> *(Pause. **GALINA** gathers the invitations.)*

Sweetheart...

> *(**GALINA** exits to bedroom and slams the door.)*

You're lucky you're going to die childless.

> *(**RAYA** looks down, presses her temples, and winces.)*

KOSTYA. You okay?

RAYA. Hm? Oh, I don't know, headache. I can't do anything right with her, lately.

KOSTYA. She's just nervous about the wedding.

> *(**RAYA** gets another pain in her head.)*

Maybe something stronger?

> *(He offers to pour her a cognac, but she holds up her tea.)*

RAYA. I'm good. Listen, I heard from Lyudmila about Chechnya.

KOSTYA. Right, I...I haven't been able to look into that.

RAYA. Kostya, I do actually have to be at my daughter's wedding, I don't want to cut it too close. Lyudmila needs the first payment for the driver and for bribes, a hundred thousand to start, and Euros, just in case. I told her next week, I can't push it off.

KOSTYA. No, I know, I've just been busy with, um... Okay. I'm not sure how much longer I'll be at *Moscow Novosti*. I had an interview last week, a job interview.

RAYA. Oh. That's great, that's wonderful. Where?

(*Beat.*)

It's impressive, isn't it? If it's too impressive, don't tell me, I'll feel terrible. No, I'm kidding, I'm good. I'm actually going to America in the fall for my book.

KOSTYA. Oh, that's great.

RAYA. Yeah, it's exciting. So. Tell me, what's the job?

KOSTYA. Television.

RAYA. Television?

KOSTYA. Too impressive?

RAYA. Television where? Europe, America, what –

KOSTYA. No. No, here. Media One. Managing Deputy Director.

(*Pause.*)

RAYA. How did that happen?

KOSTYA. You remember I know Andrei Kirov from / school, yeah, so –

RAYA. I remember.

KOSTYA. He got me an interview. I've got a second one next week, but it's looking good, very positive.

RAYA. I don't understand.

KOSTYA. Well, you put on a suit and a nice tie, they call you into a very big office. First, they offer you coffee –

RAYA. You can't work for them.

KOSTYA. I can if they hire me.

RAYA. It's state-run media.

KOSTYA. I wouldn't call it that –

RAYA. You can call it whatever you want, that's what it is.

KOSTYA. They're sympathetic to the Kremlin, but they do air opposition opinions.

RAYA. As a joke! They bring someone on to yell at them –

KOSTYA. They get on the air – People still hear them.

RAYA. You got the interview through the Kremlin's Communication Director, tell me again how it's not state-run media.

(*Beat.*)

KOSTYA. Our boss is in and out of the country as it is –

RAYA. We're still getting paychecks. You still have editorial control. You think you'll have that –

KOSTYA. For how long? How long before he ends up in London, before it's not worth the risk to publish.

RAYA. It could be years.

KOSTYA. It could be. Or it could be months.

RAYA. You're worried we'll be shut down by the government, so you're going to go work for the government. I'm not following / that line –

KOSTYA. Getting shut down is the best case scenario. The best. Don't make jokes, don't pretend you don't know that. It's a good opportunity, a very good one – It's the only thing I've ever done. Even when it was just getting coffee, copy editing, typing up releases from the Central Committee.

RAYA. That's basically what you'll be doing again.

KOSTYA. Well, at least this time I'll be getting paid for it.

RAYA. So, it's about money.

KOSTYA. It's about my life. My mother's here, my sister, my sister – She called me last week to invite me to my nephew's graduation party, they're renting a hall, she's getting a fucking ice sculpture, and I start thinking about time and how it passes and how after it's gone it's basically just about who you spent it with. And she starts to tell me the details, the address, and I cut her off. I thought, get it in person, don't let her tell you over the phone, you don't know who's listening, and if something were to happen to me, why should it ruin a good party?

(Beat.)

RAYA. You can teach. You can start writing again, about something else, sports, movies –

KOSTYA. I don't want to start writing, again.

RAYA. So, teach –

KOSTYA. It's been four years since he was appointed! Has anything we've done made a difference? Has anything you've written altered a single trajectory? It's not spiritual, it's not the priesthood, it's a job, it's just a job, can we – Let's not talk about it, let's just agree to not talk about it...

*(The oven timer beeps. **KOSTYA** turns it off.)*

RAYA. "Glasnost Will Lead to Downfall of Soviet Economy."

KOSTYA. What?

RAYA. Your first byline. *Izvestia*, 1986, they buried it in the back half.

KOSTYA. It was on page ten.

RAYA. I had never read anything that said what we were doing was wrong. There were facts, actual numbers, reasons, trains of thought that made sense.

KOSTYA. It wasn't very good.

RAYA. It was terrible, but it was *true*. I didn't even know who you were, but I knew I wanted to. Because I remember reading that, reading your words and feeling real. Isn't that insane? I didn't know I wasn't real until I saw something that was. I was thirty-two and all of a sudden, I became real.

    *(***GALINA*** enters.)*

GALINA. Did you set the table – The littlest thing – Kostya, would you get the plates?

KOSTYA. Yeah, sure.

GALINA. And wine glasses, in the second...uh-huh.

KOSTYA. I got it.

RAYA. Leave them. Leave the glasses.

GALINA. What's wrong?

RAYA. He's not staying.

GALINA. What are you talking about?

RAYA. He's not staying. Would you get his coat, please?

KOSTYA. Darling, come on –

RAYA. You take whatever job you want, you're an adult. But don't ask me to look away, to pretend, because I can't – Would you please get his fucking coat!

    *(***GALINA*** gives him his coat.)*

KOSTYA. You should wait to go to Chechnya. You shouldn't go at all, but if you are gonna go, you should wait. It's too close to the election.

GALINA. When are you going to Chechnya?

RAYA. Don't worry about it, it's not –

GALINA. When?

KOSTYA. If something happens to you, they'll bury it – It doesn't matter how many half-assed complaints they'd get from America, they won't care.

GALINA. What is he talking about?

RAYA. You starting your job early? Spiking a story before they hire you, is this part of your salary negotiation?

KOSTYA. I don't want to get a phone call from your daughter in the middle of the night – that you're missing. Or you've been shot –

GALINA. Mom –

RAYA. Then you're going to be very disappointed Kostya, because you are going to get that call.

KOSTYA. What are you saying –?

RAYA. And then you'll get a fucking lie about some kid who was trying to steal my purse and shot me in the head. And you'll have to run it over and over. And you're going to have to believe it or be very good at faking it, so why don't you start practicing now, why don't you start practicing to my face?

> (**KOSTYA** *exits.* **RAYA** *winces and holds her side. She is in pain but covering it.*)

GALINA. When were you going to tell me?

RAYA. I didn't have dates, I didn't want to worry you.

GALINA. Mom, I can't do anything when you're there. I can't think, I can't even breathe.

RAYA. I'm only going for two weeks.

GALINA. Don't. *Please don't.*

RAYA. Look, we just had an election. Nobody is talking about the war, nobody's even thinking about it, I have to go now.

GALINA. You don't have to do anything.

RAYA. Honey –

GALINA. You *want* to. Don't pretend anyone is forcing you. You're doing exactly what you want to do, just like always! God, why do I even bother?

RAYA. Sweetheart, please, let's talk about this.

GALINA. I'm going to stay with Papa.

RAYA. Galina.

GALINA. Have a great trip, maybe I'll see you at my wedding!

(**GALINA** *goes off to the bedroom.*)

RAYA. Galina! Honey, please stay, I want you to stay –

(**RAYA** *looks at her for a beat, then grabs her own abdomen and groans, doubles over.*)

Oh God, oh my God.

(**RAYA** *touches her face. Blood is coming out of her nose. She stumbles over to the table and knocks down the teacup. It shatters. She stares at it for a moment and realizes what's happening.* **GALINA** *re-enters with her suitcase.*)

GALINA. Mom?

RAYA. I'm so sorry.

GALINA. What is it?

RAYA. I didn't want you to be here for this, I really didn't, I promise.

GALINA. What's wrong?

> (**RAYA** *grabs her abdomen and coughs up a*
> *startling amount of blood.* **GALINA** *runs to*
> *her and holds her as she buckles.*)

Mom! Oh, God...

End of Part One

PART TWO

One

(In the darkness, a funeral hymn is heard.*
Somber voices soar in the blackness.)

(Projection:)   September 2004.

Terrorists attack a school in Beslan, Russia.

(A candle flickers, followed by a few more.)

3 days, 333 people dead.

186 children killed.

(The stage is awash in flickering candles.)

It started on the first day of school.

Knowledge Day.

*(Lights rise on **YEVGENY** and **RAYA** near a small shrine covered with flowers and stuffed animals. He holds a teddy bear. She holds a small bouquet of flowers. She has a scar on her throat from where she was intubated.)*

---

* A license to produce *Vladimir* does not include a performance license for any third-party or copyrighted recordings. Licensees should create their own.

YEVGENY. They keep saying on the news that less than a hundred people were killed. But my neighbor has a cousin in Kavkaz, he said they pulled out hundreds of bodies, the smell was... Do you know anything?

RAYA. The numbers didn't make sense. There were almost a thousand students, plus teachers, parents dropping them off, so – That's nonsense. And I wouldn't be surprised if we killed most of them.

YEVGENY. What?

RAYA. Not on purpose, just ineptitude.

    (Beat.)

YEVGENY. I heard about what happened to you, I'm sorry.

RAYA. Sorry I was poisoned, or sorry that I recovered and you still have to deal with me?

    (Beat.)

YEVGENY. A little of both.

Do they know who did it?

RAYA. They questioned my ex-husband for eight hours, said it was probably a crime of passion. I told them that was literally impossible.

YEVGENY. On Media One they said it was some Chechen warlord.

RAYA. Do you believe that?

    (Beat.)

YEVGENY. No.

    *(**YEVGENY** places the teddy bear on the shrine.)*

I was looking at Katya this morning. She was still asleep, and I got this flash. I pictured her there. She'd already had the baby, he's older, it's his first day of school. I see him in his uniform, flower for the teacher, then her lying on top of him. Her hand over his little skull. Both of them so scared.

> (**RAYA** *looks around, makes sure no one is watching, and pulls an envelope out of her bag. She hands it to* **YEVGENY**, *who starts to open it.*)

RAYA. Put it in your coat.

> (*He blanches, unused to covert operations, quickly puts the envelope away.*)

My guy at the Tax Authority pulled files. I found the shell companies, but I can't figure out who's behind them. That's a list.

YEVGENY. Okay. I got the tax ID. When I ran it, there were refunds deposited in banks all over the country. And then wired out of the accounts almost immediately. The deposits were small, but they add up.

RAYA. To how much?

YEVGENY. Twenty million rubles.

RAYA. We have to trace it... You have to call the banks and find out who withdrew the money. Or go visit them in person, that's how you find the connection.

YEVGENY. Me?

RAYA. Your boss will pay for it, won't he? I can try but my new editor is cheap. And scared. It's a shit combination. I can't show up, I can't even use my name right now. No one will talk to me.

YEVGENY. You really think I should go?

RAYA. Yes.

> (**YEVGENY** *seems unsure.*)

Are you backing out?

YEVGENY. No, it's just –

RAYA. If you're going to back out, tell me now.

YEVGENY. I'm not saying that, it's just –

RAYA. What?

YEVGENY. This! Everything! It feels like too much is happening. Who even thinks of something like this? Attacking a school. These people are monsters.

RAYA. They're not monsters. They're people who have never been treated like human beings, and then we expect they'll act like human beings.

YEVGENY. This is why they hate you.

RAYA. They hate me because I won't say, "Heroes of the Russian Federation / sacrificing their lives –"

YEVGENY. I'm not talking about the Kremlin, I'm talking about people. My cousin, my dad – My dad hates you. Once he gets going, "that goddamn…"

RAYA. Bitch.

YEVGENY. "Let her leave if she hates this country, go live in the mountains, shit in a pot, if she has so much respect for those people." I'm all for context, but not when –

RAYA. But not when it implicates you?

YEVGENY. Some things are just wrong.

RAYA. Yes, but that doesn't mean they're simple. This is how they get them, people like your father. Us good, them bad, no nuance, no reflection. Not a single person willing to say, "Okay, but why?" I'm sorry, but the world is more complicated than that.

YEVGENY. You think so?

RAYA. You don't?

YEVGENY. What if you're spending your life looking for reasons, perspective, how everybody ended up the way they ended up, and while you're doing that, the other people are running the world, because they understand something you don't.

RAYA. Us good, them bad?

YEVGENY. They understand you have to decide what you believe and fight for it. No questions, no second guessing –

RAYA. Whatever the cost.

YEVGENY. Whatever the cost.

RAYA. So, if you have to walk into a school with a rifle and ten kilos of dynamite strapped to your chest, well, you're a freedom fighter, right? No questions, no second-guessing.

YEVGENY. ...God, you're annoying.

RAYA. We should go.

(She starts to leave, then stops.)

If you want to stop working with me on this, you can. If you need to go back to your life, I'll understand.

YEVGENY. When did you become so understanding?

RAYA. I've...I've had a rough couple of weeks. Look, I'm not saying I won't judge you and think much less of you, but if you need an out...I'm giving you an out.

(Bcat.)

YEVGENY. I'll start calling banks tomorrow.

Two

(*A* **NEWS PERSONALITY** *talks directly to the camera, as the crew films him.* **KOSTYA** *is off to the side, supervising.* **ANDREI** *enters at some point during the following, observing.*)

NEWS PERSONALITY. It's ridiculous when you think about it – But this is the way to make people believe. You come up with something so absurd, they think you couldn't invent that. It *has* to be true – The government *knew*? They *knew* that a school was going to be attacked – That children were going to be used as human shields, and they did nothing? Okay, so a Chechen terrorist is claiming the Kremlin got a warning – Now we're supposed to trust the word of terrorists, but all right – What did this clown say – Anna? What'd he say, a few... (*An off-camera voice murmurs.*) four? Anna says four – Our government got four hours notice and did nothing? Well, look, if you believe that, you're a goddamn moron. Our government is *that* sinister. It's a little too convenient, if you ask me, it fits the terrorist's narrative a little too – Jesus fuck! You're sure there's nothing? Look! Right here. I can feel it, right now, I'm feeling it with my tongue.

(*He bares his teeth and points between two of them.*)

CREW MEMBER. I don't see anything.

NEWS PERSONALITY. So what am I, fucking delusional?!

CREW MEMBER. No?

NEWS PERSONALITY. It's like a piece of corn, it's killing me...

KOSTYA. Can someone get him a toothpick?

NEWS PERSONALITY. Thank God – This is what I was talking about, Kostya, the incompetence, the lack of support.

CREW MEMBER. I have floss, is that okay?

NEWS PERSONALITY. New people every week, every show we're starting from zero.

KOSTYA. Right.

NEWS PERSONALITY. I can't be concerned with minutia.

KOSTYA. Definitely.

NEWS PERSONALITY. It's systemic – I don't even know if it can change.

KOSTYA. Mmm.

CREW MEMBER. *(Holding out floss.)* Is this –?

NEWS PERSONALITY. Just put it on the desk.

(**CREW MEMBER** *leaves the floss and recedes.*)

KOSTYA. You know, I think the issue is depletion. What you do is so hard, the amount of energy required – There's only so much space in one's mind, and you are so clearly using all of it.

NEWS PERSONALITY. I really am.

KOSTYA. Listen, I'm grateful for how honest you're being. Because now it's on me. Let me carry this, so you can do what you're best at, what millions of people tune in to see you do every week. Can you do that?

NEWS PERSONALITY. Of course I can do that, I'm a professional.

KOSTYA. No question. Why don't we take a minute, re-center, we'll work on Alexei and come back.

(Beat.)

NEWS PERSONALITY. Yeah, all right.

KOSTYA. Okay, great. Let's take five and then reset...

> (*The* **CREW** *begin resetting as* **KOSTYA** *lights a cigarette.* **ANDREI** *approaches.*)

ANDREI. Well done.

KOSTYA. Fuck you.

ANDREI. That was masterful.

KOSTYA. Seriously, bend over that box, so I can shove my foot up your ass.

ANDREI. How's it going?

KOSTYA. Fantastic, I'm like a jockey but I've got to make sure the horse feels really good about himself.

ANDREI. Sveta wants you to come for dinner. She's convinced you're spending all your time drunk and alone.

KOSTYA. And she wants to ruin all my fun.

ANDREI. You should come. Misha's home from university, we're having friends over – people you should meet. Now you're settling in, it's about time.

KOSTYA. Yeah, I'll, uh... I'll let you know.

ANDREI. Okay... So? What is it, what did you want to talk about?

KOSTYA. Well, I uh, I had an idea.

ANDREI. Good for you.

KOSTYA. I had an idea for a segment and I took it to the network, but they weren't totally comfortable with it. They needed some assurance.

ANDREI. Assurance.

KOSTYA. They wanted to know we'd be covered.

(Beat.)

ANDREI. What's your idea?

KOSTYA. There have been all kinds of rumors. About the attack, what we knew, what we didn't know, *when* we knew it, and I was thinking what we're doing now, the denial, the sort of blanket denial is not as effective as you guys were hoping it would be.

ANDREI. Uh-huh.

KOSTYA. I think we need a proactive approach, I think if we had someone on, someone trusted who could attest to the fact that this was a terrible tragedy, the casualties were horrifying, but none of this was due to um, you know to negligence, I think that would go a long way.

ANDREI. Kostya, what the fuck are you talking about?

KOSTYA. I think we should have Raisa Bobrinskaya on.

> *(**ANDREI** laughs.)*

Just on one of the panels, her and a few other guests, maybe Agnessa Kirlova, I know you guys love her. Look, people know Raya doesn't spew the party line –

ANDREI. Yeah, no shit.

KOSTYA. They would believe her if she said there was no prior knowledge. That you guys didn't get a warning that there would be an attack on a school and fucking ignore it.

ANDREI. Are you having some kind of psychotic break?

KOSTYA. We've had people on, expressing the opposition view.

ANDREI. People. Not her.

KOSTYA. This would be the same thing. She is clearly against the war, can you imagine if she comes out in support of the rescue operation?

ANDREI. No. I can't, because she would never do it.

KOSTYA. She would if it was true.

ANDREI. Bullshit.

KOSTYA. Unless it's not true. Are you saying it's not true? That the Kremlin received a warning about a terrorist attack on children and sat on it for four hours?

ANDREI. ...What the fuck are you doing?

KOSTYA. Because if that's true, if that's what happened... I don't fucking understand you.

ANDREI. What I'm about to say is not a threat. It's not a warning. It's just what's gonna happen. You're going to go back to your office and tell your secretary that you're not feeling well and you need to go home early. And then you're gonna go to your apartment, and you will never. Ever. Talk about this again. Because if you do, you will lose your job, you will lose your life, you will lose everything.

> (**ANDREI** *starts to go and* **KOSTYA** *gets in his way.*)

KOSTYA. When we had drinks that night, did you know she was going to be poisoned?

ANDREI. Kostya.

KOSTYA. We're friends, you can tell me.

ANDREI. You need to stop.

KOSTYA. It's just between us, two old friends, did you know? Did you fucking know?!

ANDREI. What does it matter if I knew?! It's not like you would've done anything about it!

> (*After a moment,* **KOSTYA** *lunges at him.*)

Get off!

*(They struggle like middle-aged men who aren't used to physical altercations. **ANDREI** manages to knee **KOSTYA**. **KOSTYA** curls up in pain.)*

Fuck! I gotta tell you, as much as I hate her, people like you are even worse. People who think they're better, so pure, meanwhile look where you're fucking working! You were always that guy, Kostya. I remember you hiding cassettes in the dormitory, Vysotsky, The Stones. I thought you were so brave – I thought people like you would remake this country, but you're actually the ones who keep it running. All the corruption – it needs people who think they're above it. Who rebel in quiet, meaningless ways without sacrificing a fucking thing.

KOSTYA. So, that's the way you work it in your head. That you're a hero. When you're just some hick from the Urals who swindled his way past the front gate.

ANDREI. You feel like you let off some steam?

KOSTYA. Just fire me, you son of a bitch, just fucking fire me.

ANDREI. I'm not your boss.

KOSTYA. Then have me fired.

(Beat.)

ANDREI. No. I'm not gonna do that.

Go home, Kostya. You and I both know, now that you've had your little moment, you're going to fold up all your brave thoughts and put them away where they can't get you in trouble.

KOSTYA. No...

ANDREI. Really? We'll see.

*(**ANDREI** exits, leaving **KOSTYA** alone.)*

Three

(*Raya's apartment.* **RAYA** *enters, takes off
her coat, flips through mail, etc. Behind her,
a* **FIGURE** *in black, wearing a balaclava,
carrying a rifle, passes through the hallway.*
RAYA *presses the button on the answering
machine.*)

GALINA. (*Voice on the answering machine.*) Hey it's me,
I'm just out running an errand. I'll be back soon to take
you to physical therapy. Okay, I love you. Charge your
phone.

(*The* **FIGURE** *in black appears behind* **RAYA**
*as she makes a cup of tea. This time from a
box in her purse. Next message.*)

KOSTYA. (*Voice on the answering machine.*) Hey, it's
Kostya, just calling to see if you'll pick up. Galina
said you were doing much better. I badgered her into
telling me, don't be mad. Um... I miss you... Hey, why
do women watch porn until the end? To see if they get
married.

(**RAYA** *laughs.*)

FIGURE. You're not nervous about the tea?

(*She turns around and is startled by the*
FIGURE *in black. They look at each other for a
moment. The* **FIGURE** *removes her balaclava.
It's* **CHOVKA**.)

CHOVKA. I guess they can kill you any way they want.
Polonium, Novichok, pushed from a window, bullet to
the head.

RAYA. I don't want to see you anymore.

CHOVKA. And yet here we are.

RAYA. Fuck... Why are you wearing that?

CHOVKA. Do you like it?

RAYA. Why are you wearing that?!

CHOVKA. I think you know why.

RAYA. Were you there? Did you hurt those children? Were you there?

CHOVKA. You know, I really have to thank you. That first time we met, I said nobody cared about us. Do you remember what you said? You said I had to make it so people couldn't look away. No one's looking away now.

RAYA. That's not what I meant.

CHOVKA. You said you would change the channel, because it was too depressing. But what if you couldn't? What if the story was so big it was on every channel?

RAYA. I never meant you had the right to kill people –

CHOVKA. Why? Why don't I have that right? Why don't our lives count as much as yours?

RAYA. They do, they count –

CHOVKA. We're just numbers, we're numbers of corpses that tick, tick, tick, tick, meanwhile you get to be a person.

RAYA. That's why I wrote about you, to make people care. I'm helping!

CHOVKA. You really think a lot of yourself, don't you?

RAYA. I don't.

CHOVKA. What a hero you are.

RAYA. I meant I'm being useful, what I'm doing is important –

CHOVKA. Oh, it is, I never would have done this if not for you. It's like you said, I'm not a monster, I'm something you created.

RAYA. No, that's not – I meant there's a reason behind the brutality and you have to find the context.

CHOVKA. What does finding the context do? Absolve you of blame?

RAYA. Stop arguing with me, you're just say things, you're just saying words, and they don't mean anything!

CHOVKA. We have a lot in common.

RAYA. All I did was tell people who you are, and try to make them care. I'm helping, I'm doing something useful, I am –

CHOVKA. You gave us a voice –

RAYA. This isn't my fault!

CHOVKA. Made us believe we had power.

RAYA. This isn't my fault, it isn't!

(**GALINA** *enters, as* **CHOVKA** *exits.*)

GALINA. Mom?

(**GALINA** *looks around, confused at whom her mother was yelling at.*)

Four

*(Jim's apartment. Night. A loud pounding on
the door.* **JIM** *enters in his boxers.)*

YEVGENY. *(Knocking.)* Hello? Jim?

JIM. Yevgeny?

YEVGENY. Yeah, it's me!

JIM. Jesus –

*(**JIM** opens the door. **YEVGENY** is disheveled
and out of breath.)*

I think you gave me a fucking heart attack.

YEVGENY. I have to talk to you and I didn't want to use
phone. *(Tries to catch his breath.)* Sorry, I coming from
office – I think someone following me, so I run last few
blocks, then he run too and he was fast – Wow, this
apartment, oofa. This yours, you own?

JIM. Yeah – Why were you being followed?

YEVGENY. They tell you who was living here when it was
built?

JIM. What – No.

YEVGENY. Sometimes they tell you. If person was high
enough. This belong to someone important for sure.

*(**MASHA** enters, wearing one of Jim's shirts
and nothing else.)*

MASHA. *(With accent.)* Jim, what is going on?

YEVGENY. Oh. I'm sorry.

JIM. It's okay.

YEVGENY. I didn't think you would have, eh –

JIM. Don't worry about it.

MASHA. *(To* **YEVGENY**, *no accent.)* What's the matter with you?

YEVGENY. *(No accent.)* I'm sorry.

MASHA. *(No accent.)* It's two o'clock in the morning, you're pounding on the door, what's someone supposed to think? What would you think if someone was pounding on your door?

YEVGENY. *(No accent.)* I don't know.

MASHA. *(No accent.)* Yes you do, because you're not a fucking idiot. You can't do that to someone.

YEVGENY. *(No accent.)* I'm sorry.

MASHA. *(No accent.)* You can't do that.

JIM. Masha?

MASHA. *(With accent.)* Sorry, I...was scared.

JIM. Oh.

MASHA. *(With accent.)* I was just scared.

JIM. There's um, sleeping pills in the medicine cabinet. Would that help? Turn on the radio, something relaxing. I'll be in in a minute.

> *(They share an intimate moment.* **YEVGENY** *looks away.* **MASHA** *exits.* **YEVGENY** *speaks with an accent for the remainder of the scene.)*

You want some water.

YEVGENY. Is okay. This better, I think.

> *(He picks up a decanter of liquor.)*

JIM. Go ahead.

I don't normally... *(He motions toward the bedroom where* **MASHA** *exited.)* ...with employees. Things have been complicated at home. I'd appreciate if you didn't mention anything.

YEVGENY. Of course.

JIM.   Thank you. Why do you think you were being followed –

YEVGENY. I found him. I found who stole the money.

JIM. You're fucking kidding me.

YEVGENY. You knowing what is delphin? Is living in water, big animal.

JIM. Dolphin?

YEVGENY. I think yeah, same thing. This who stole your name. Mafia guy, Georgian. The Dolphin.

JIM. That's gotta be the worst criminal name I've ever heard. Why not the Piranha, the fuckin' Shark.

YEVGENY. Probably there is already Shark, maybe more than one. This is very common evil fish.

JIM. What happened, how did you find him?

YEVGENY. I was able to match deposits to Dmitri Sokolov, the Dolphin – But. Here is interesting part. Address for Sokolov's companies are in little nothing city. And when I call them for more information, they tell me I need to speak with someone in Ministry of Finance.

JIM. Why would the Finance Ministry...

YEVGENY. Be handling company belonging to mafia – I think this is good question, also. So I call Finance Ministry. Man say, "I think is better you don't call back, Yevgeny."

(Beat.)

I never give him my name.

JIM. Fuck.

YEVGENY. I know.

JIM. And someone followed you here.

YEVGENY. Yeah.

JIM. Fuck.

YEVGENY. Listen, I know someone who is working for newspaper, journalist. She is interested in this type of story. I wanted to tell you first so you know, but think is best I contact now.

JIM. Go to the press – Why don't I just report it?

YEVGENY. Who you reporting to?

JIM. To the Tax Authority.

YEVGENY. Jim. Tax Authority reports to Minister of Finance. This the boss. You don't go to clerk, tell him owner of store is stealing and expect something will be done.

JIM. So, you're saying we go straight to the press and say the Russian government embezzled millions in taxpayer money.

YEVGENY. And best part, we have proof.

(**JIM** *pours himself a drink and downs it.*)

JIM. You're sure?

YEVGENY. Positive.

JIM. Okay. Okay. Well. This is good work. This is why I hired you, the attention to detail, how you're willing to go A to Z in a totally creative – This is excellent stuff, man. Really good.

YEVGENY. Thank you.

JIM. Yeah, man, you're welcome. So, uh, so let me get you a taxi.

YEVGENY. Um...

JIM. Or use my car. What am I thinking, of course, use my car.

YEVGENY. Jim, wait – I have to tell you, I think is better we releasing information soon. I promise you, this is going all the way up.

JIM. I don't give a shit if it's going to the fucking moon.

YEVGENY. You want me to find out who is stealing your name, using your company –

JIM. And you did. And I'm thanking you and providing you with a very comfortable ride back to your apartment.

YEVGENY. I don't understand.

JIM. I thought we were dealing with some thug in a sweat suit and a gold chain, not the fucking president. What do you think will happen if we go public? What do you think will happen to your job, to your life? 'Cause I know what'll happen to mine. I lose my operating license, I lose whatever money I have here – My clients will run away as fast as fuck.

YEVGENY. You are one who is telling me be a lion. What 'bout you, you are lion, too, no?

JIM. In theory, sure.

YEVGENY. What this mean, "in theory"?

JIM. I'm not blowing up my life, Yevgeny. I've spent years stacking one shit brick on top of another – I'm sorry, but I have a business, I have a home, kids – I have a family.

YEVGENY. Also don't forget you have a secretary.

(*Beat.*)

JIM. You wouldn't be the first person to look the other way.

YEVGENY. You ever think what happen in this place before you living here? You ever think of man who used to lie where you lying now, who was looking at same ceiling, same walls, you never think of what he do to live in such beautiful home? Head of secret police used to bury young girls in his wife's rose garden.

JIM. I'm not burying anyone in a fucking rose garden.

YEVGENY. No, you're just enjoying the view.

> (**YEVGENY** *starts to go.*)

JIM. Anything you found using your work computer, your Blackberry, any digital record belongs to the company, and I am not authorizing you to share it.

> (**YEVGENY** *laughs.*)

I will fire you.

YEVGENY. Okay.

JIM. Yevgeny!

Take the car. If someone's following you, you should take the car. Please. Take the car.

> (**YEVGENY** *exits.* **MASHA** *appears in the doorway.*)

MASHA. *(With accent.)* What is wrong with him?

JIM. No idea. Let's go back to bed.

Five

(Morning. Raya's apartment. **YEVGENY** *knocks and* **RAYA** *lets him in.)*

YEVGENY. Sorry it took so long, I finally lost the guy.

RAYA. Don't talk next to the kitchen, it's where they put the bug.

YEVGENY. How do you know?

RAYA. They've put one there before.

YEVGENY. You think they're dumb enough to put it in the same place twice?

RAYA. Yeah.

(They sit on the other side of the apartment.)

YEVGENY. I found the money. I found out who took the money.

RAYA. How high does it go?

YEVGENY. High.

What's our next step? That's everything. I took it with me, just in case. You said your boss is scared, but you must have connections, I'm sure someone will run it.

(Beat.)

RAYA. This will get back to you.

YEVGENY. What?

RAYA. You've been asking questions and someone followed you. If I write the story, they'll know you're my source.

YEVGENY. You and I both knew they'd figure out I was your source from day one.

RAYA. Well, on day one I thought it was worth it. Now, I'm not so sure.

YEVGENY. It doesn't matter, no one has to figure anything out. I want you to name me. I want to go on the record.

RAYA. No you don't.

YEVGENY. I do.

RAYA. No. You don't.

YEVGENY. I found this. And you have to write it, because if you don't, it never happened. And if I don't put my name on it, it's like I don't care. But I do. And I'm sick of pretending I don't. These people take everything they want. Any time they want it. And we think if we keep quiet, maybe they'll leave us alone, maybe we can just live our lives, but I'm sick of it. It's sickening. I want you to use my name.

RAYA. I'm not going to do it. *No.* If I write this story, nothing will change. No one will get arrested, no one will be charged. And that's fine, that's my job. But I am *not* dragging another person into it. I don't want to be responsible for you.

YEVGENY. But you are responsible for me. If I never met you, I'd never have done this, I'd have let it go. Like we all let it go. This is going to sound stupid, but I feel brave. And it feels good, it's a good feeling.

RAYA. Zhenya...you're about to have a baby.

YEVGENY. I already had a baby.

RAYA. What? When?

YEVGENY. Three weeks ago. A girl.

RAYA. Oh, my God.

YEVGENY. Here...

(He shows her a picture from his wallet.)

Yelena.

RAYA. Oh, she's huge… she's beautiful. Don't do this to yourself. You're going to want to be around for her. Trust me, she's going to amaze you.

YEVGENY. I do trust you.

> *(Beat.)*

RAYA. I think something is wrong with me. I don't feel like myself, I know what's right and what's wrong, but I don't know that it matters. I keep hoping this place will change, but what if it never does? What if we're not capable of change, what if the best we can do is slightly less awful? …I don't know if I can do this anymore.

YEVGENY. Well. Someone has to.

> *(He leaves the documents, and exits.)*

Six

(**GALINA** *enters a dressing room in the
catering hall in her wedding dress. She looks,
finds a pack of cigarettes, lights one, inhaling
deeply.* **RAYA** *enters, dressed for the wedding.*)

RAYA. What are you doing, people are asking me where
you are.

GALINA. I just needed a minute.

RAYA. Okay.

GALINA. Mom.

RAYA. Yes.

GALINA. That woman is a cunt.

RAYA. I know.

GALINA. I don't want her in my life.

RAYA. Yep.

GALINA. And Sasha never says anything, he just tells me
to ignore her. I've lost respect for him.

RAYA. That's totally normal.

GALINA. I don't want that to be normal.

RAYA. Listen to me, he's going to realize very soon, that
he would much rather please you than her.

GALINA. Did Daddy ever feel that way about you?

RAYA. That's not a fair comparison.

GALINA. You're just placating me.

RAYA. I'm not!

GALINA. You want me to marry him, so you won't have
to deal with the caterers.

RAYA. You can't compare you and Sasha to me and your father, because you're better than I am. You are genuinely good. You…you care about everyone, in the smallest moments, you care about people. Since you were a little girl, you've always *always* had this ability to make everyone around you feel so important. So loved. You didn't get it from either of us. It's like when two ugly people make a beautiful child, genetic mystery, but it happened with you.

GALINA. Mom.

RAYA. Hm?

GALINA. I want you to stop.

RAYA. Stop what?

GALINA. You know what.

RAYA. Oh, honey…

GALINA. Promise me.

Promise me you'll get old.

And you'll meet my children.

And we'll get together on holidays and birthdays.

And that I'll be able to call you. Whenever, even if it's just to listen to myself talk.

And that I'll get to watch you turn into your mother and never know where your keys are.

RAYA. I don't know where my keys are right now.

GALINA. Promise.

I want to be your age and still know you. Still be able to touch you.

I want to see your skin get papery and thin.

I want to stand next to you forty years from now and hold your hand while you slip away, And I want my daughter to be holding your other hand.

GALINA. I want her to know you.

Promise me...

Mom...

Promise me.

(*Beat.*)

RAYA. You have to go.

(**GALINA** *nods. Transition to the ceremony.* **RAYA** *moves to watch from one side as* **KOSTYA** *enters.*)

(**CHOIR** *parts are sung by actors onstage other than* **DEACON**, *as well as offstage actors. Pre-recorded singing is also an option.*)

CHOIR. Lord have mercy.

(*The* **DEACON** *places a crown on* **SASHA**'s *head.*)

DEACON. The servant of God, Alexander, is crowned unto the handmaiden of God, Galina, in the name of the Father, and of the Son, and of the Holy Spirit.

CHOIR. Amen.

(*The* **DEACON** *places a crown on* **GALINA**'s *head.*)

DEACON. The handmaiden of God, Galina, is crowned unto the servant of God, Alexander, in the name of the Father, and of the Son, and of the Holy Spirit.

CHOIR. Amen.

Glory to Thee, O Lord, Glory to Thee!

(*The* **CHOIR** *continues singing as the procession walks offstage, leaving* **RAYA** *alone with* **KOSTYA**.)

KOSTYA. I did get an invitation. And it wasn't rescinded, so technically, I'm a legitimate, if totally unwelcome guest. You look good.

RAYA. I look like shit.

KOSTYA. Yeah, but well polished. Are you okay?

RAYA. Why, are you reporting back to your boss? She looked good, might want to up the dosage next time.

KOSTYA. For fuck's sake, I would never hurt you, you know that.

RAYA. I don't know what I know anymore.

KOSTYA. Okay, fine. You said you were leaving for your book tour after the wedding. I'm assuming you'll be in New York?

RAYA. It's the last stop.

KOSTYA. So, in about a month?

RAYA. Just about, yeah.

KOSTYA. Good, well, I contacted a friend, she can set up meetings once you get there. I don't have much pull anymore, obviously, but she's at Reuters, she knows everyone.

RAYA. What are you talking about?

KOSTYA. She'll reach out to people for you. For a job.

RAYA. I have a job.

KOSTYA. You... Raya, they are not going to chance it next time. They will kill you.

RAYA. Did they send you to tell me that?

KOSTYA. Nobody sent me to tell you anything. God, you're so fucking arrogant. I'm begging you, please – Please do not make me mourn you, I don't think I could do it.

RAYA. You're being very dramatic.

KOSTYA. My best friend was nearly assassinated. Yes, I'm being dramatic!

RAYA. What am I supposed to do, Kostya? Get an apartment God knows where, yell at the Kremlin from five thousand miles away? Like that's going to make a difference?

KOSTYA. And you're making a difference now?

RAYA. At least I'm being annoying. And loud. It must be worth something or they wouldn't have tried offing me in the first place.

KOSTYA. Has it ever occurred to you that you won't be able to change a thing if you're not alive to do it? Okay, yes, you won't have a Russian audience. And you probably won't feel as important. But you'd still be working.

RAYA. You think I do this to feel important?

KOSTYA. I think it's part of it. Yeah, I do.

RAYA. Fuck you, Kostya.

KOSTYA. Fine, fuck me.

RAYA. The only reason I'm still doing this, *the only reason*, is because no one else is. Are you going to listen to someone tell you how their son was shot in the head with his hands tied behind his back? Are you going to sit with a girl while she tells you she was raped only she doesn't have the word for it? I don't think you want to do that Kostya, because the truth is I don't want to do it. I want to be done with it. I want to wake up in the morning, drink my coffee and be fucking done with it.

(*Pause.*)

You know what he's doing? He's making it so we can't tell which way is up, like a pilot, you know, when they can't find the horizon? Just total confusion. And numbness. Until you feel like there's nothing you can do, so you just do nothing.

KOSTYA. You can still do good work. I really believe that.

RAYA. You need to believe that because you know you never will.

KOSTYA. ...You're right. One day, I'll be an old man sitting on a folding chair in front of my apartment. I'll have been here for so long that I'll be afraid of who they tell me to be afraid of, I'll hate who they tell me to hate. I'll believe only what I see with my own eyes, and sometimes I won't even believe that. I'll be my father.

RAYA. No, you won't. Because you'll know. You'll know they're lying and stealing and killing. You'll never be able to turn that part of yourself off. And it's going to eat you up. It's going to eat you up from the inside, can't you see that? It'll be worse than being dead.

KOSTYA. Tell me that again in thirty years. We'll see if you're right.

> (**KOSTYA** *comes close. He kisses her. It's a goodbye.*)

You cannot come back here. Listen to me. You cannot come back here.

> (*He exits, leaving* **RAYA** *alone.*)

Seven

(A clap of thunder and the sound of rain.)

(Projection:)   New York City.

A disappointing bookstore.

(An easel with a large photo of a book cover, From the Graveyard: Stories of Chechnya *by Raisa Bobrinskaya, is set up next to a podium. A* **CLERK** *approaches the podium to speak. The microphone is not on and she is barely audible.)*

CLERK. *(Reads from notes.)* Good evening, thank you for joining us. It is my honor to welcome renowned Russian journalist and author Raisa Bobrinskaya. Ms. Bobrinskaya has received awards. *(To someone offstage.)* Oh, it's not? ...Okay, one sec... *(She finds the switch and turns on the mic.)* How about now? Oh yeah. Sorry, it's my first time...with a podium. I'll go back. Ms. Bobrinskaya has received awards from Amnesty International, PEN International, the Columbia School of Journalism and many others. In her eight years reporting from Chechnya, she has been the victim of countless threats. She has been arrested, kidnapped, and she was recently the target of a poisoning, which thankfully, she survived, uh... Which is great. Ms. Bobrinskaya's latest book, *From the Graveyard: Stories of Chechnya* is a searing portrait of a war that has claimed the lives of tens of thousands of civilians. It is a window into a democracy in freefall. It is a brave and defiant piece of journalism. Please join me in welcoming Raisa Bobrinskaya.

*(***RAYA*** *approaches the podium and the* **CLERK** *exits.* **RAYA** *takes a sip from a bottle of water. She speaks with an accent for the remainder of the scene.)*

RAYA. *(Speaking to offstage* **CLERK**.*)* You have cold? This not cold, you having cold?

(There is some murmuring offstage.)

Okay, forget, is fine.

CLERK. *(Offstage.)* Are you sure?

RAYA. It has to be, so yeah, is fine. Eh, thank you for this kind words.

This is from the prologue.

(She reads from her book:)

"What struck me first about the girl was her expression. It was a mixture of petulance and rage. I thought of the times my daughter looked at me this way. And then I thought of this girl. She was waiting alone by the side of the road, a dangerous proposition for a woman in Chechnya..."

(There is a pounding on a door. **RAYA** *is the only one who hears it.)*

Excuse me... "A dangerous proposition for..."

(More pounding. A light finds **YEVGENY** *in the distance. He wears a prison jumpsuit, head shaved. He writes a letter.)*

(To the audience.) Sorry, I am now traveling for few weeks, talking about what's happening in my country, and eh, I'm supposed to go back tomorrow. I have ticket, flight from JFK, and everyone asking, my friends, my agent, people like you in audience, they ask: Are you afraid to go back? And they don't say of who. They don't use his name. Only, how can you go back? Aren't you afraid?

And it make me so...*mad,*

That one man should have such power,

RAYA. One. Small. Not great intellectual, not insightful,

Only talent is finding ugliness and knowing how to use it.

And yet this little man take up so much space.

And I'm thinking...

I don't want to give this man such power.

He does not deserve such power.

And maybe it's nothing what I'm doing, it is simple act by simple person.

(**YEVGENY** *speaks as he folds up and seals his letter. No accent.*)

YEVGENY. I don't know that you'll ever read this, but I know you'll want to. You'll want to know everything that happened, and you won't stop until you find out. Because you're annoying.

(**RAYA** *laughs as though she can hear him.*)

So, here you go.

When they finally came to the door, they were there all day. Emptying drawers, cutting open pillowcases, and one of them got hungry, an older guy – And he was eating the kholodets Katya's mother made, just standing at the fridge eating, and I wanted to smash his face into the window.

RAYA. Maybe this is only weapon we have, simple acts done by simple people. And it's not deadly, this weapon. But I think, *I think*...it's very dangerous. Little men are very frightened of it.

YEVGENY. I wish I could tell you I knew, like I was a hero, but it was so...incremental. The arrest, the appeals – I kept thinking, I'll be out next week, next month. And because it was gradual, it all felt kind of...workable.

Even the interrogations. Hours, they kept badgering me to say it was a lie. That Jim had stolen the money, that I had, that it never happened – Anything would do. Except the truth.

RAYA. And maybe only way to survive the cruelty done by these little men is to believe it is an opportunity.

YEVGENY. Katya and my mother would stand outside the court building and wave at me. And they'd bring Yelena.

RAYA. How human can you be?

YEVGENY. My daughter.

RAYA. How much will you let yourself feel?

YEVGENY. They were so beautiful it hurt.

RAYA. There is saying we have in Russian, "Where you are born, this where you are useful." I am born someplace where air is so cold you can see it float above ground. I am born in land where old women gather you in their arm and it is quiet and safe. I am born in place which understands deepest part of soul, because this is where music is born, where art comes from, where literature is made to speak.

YEVGENY. It's late...and so quiet. A while ago, several men came into my cell. One of them chains my hand to the bed. They have rubber batons. I leave my body and watch them do their work. They crack ribs and shatter bones...

And I think of the day I'll be free.

RAYA. Why go back, why work and fight, why dream, why hope, why love...

YEVGENY. I'll open the front door, and see my daughter and she will light up.

RAYA. I think because it's where I was born.

YEVGENY. And we will laugh and cry.

RAYA. It's where I'm useful.

YEVGENY. And cry and laugh.

RAYA. It's worth it.

YEVGENY. I'll be home.

RAYA. It's my home.

End of Play

AFTERWORD

Since Vladimir Putin assumed the presidency, dozens of Russian journalists have been murdered or died prematurely, under questionable circumstances. Over ninety percent of these cases remain unsolved. At least seventeen journalists have been killed while covering the Russian invasion of Ukraine, and dozens more have been injured, abducted, or disappeared.

The play is a work of fiction, however the character of Raya was partly inspired by Anna Politkovskaya. Anna was a journalist and human rights activist who was critical of the Putin regime. She reported on human rights abuses by the Russian military in Chechnya. She condemned the Putin regime for dragging the country back into what she called "the Soviet abyss." She was also highly critical of Putin-installed Chechen dictator Ramzan Kadyrov. Anna was arrested, questioned, and threatened with death and rape on several occasions. Multiple attempts were made on her life. She was poisoned in 2004 on her way to aid in hostage negotiations during the Beslan school siege. On October 7, 2006, Anna was found dead in the elevator of her apartment building. She was shot several times, including once in the head at point-blank range. She was murdered on Vladimir Putin's fifty-fourth birthday. Six men were eventually charged and convicted of Anna's murder, but the person who ordered the killing remains unknown.

The character of Yevgeny was inspired by Sergei Magnitsky. Sergei was a tax auditor who worked for the law firm Firestone Duncan. In 2008 he uncovered massive tax fraud perpetrated by Russian officials. He was arrested and accused of colluding with American hedge fund manager Bill Browder to embezzle millions of dollars in tax rebates. Sergei was detained for 358 days. The Moscow Helsinki Group, a human rights organization, determined that he had been tortured and beaten to death by several officers. Sergei was tried posthumously and found guilty of tax evasion.

Since Sergei's death, Bill Browder has campaigned for the Magnitsky Act, a bill which authorizes the US and other governments to freeze assets and deny entry to individuals deemed human rights abusers. Browder was tried in Russia in absentia and found guilty of tax evasion.

In 2016 Vladimir Putin offered President Trump access to Russian Intelligence officials indicted in connection with DNC hacks, in exchange for allowing Russia to interrogate Bill Browder.

President Trump referred to this proposition as "a great offer."

As of 2025, the United States has fallen to fifty-seventh in the world for press freedom.

Citations

The Prologue:

The Old Man's resignation speech is culled from various translations of Boris Yeltsin's farewell address, broadcast December 31, 1999.

Scene Three:

I found the jokes Yevgeny and Raya tell by searching several websites and anthologies for Soviet-era jokes. None of these jokes were credited, however compilations are available for purchase, including *Forbidden Laughter: Soviet Underground Jokes* by Emil Draitser.